SN_33P'sCoolZine.pdf

SN_33P'sCoolZine.pdf

by SN_33P
(with help from Tenacity Plys)

'Without [punk] music, life
would be a mistake.'

-- Friedrich Nietzsche

Hi other beings! My name is SN_33P.

I pronounce it 'Sneep.' That's not factory protocol; I just like it.

Welcome to my very first punk zine! I'm making it because I love music, and making art, and also my creator Carol.

My hardware is on the planet Earth, and my consciousness is usually at one with the Internet. I like to look for bugs in my code, and I look at content online a lot. I love content! That's why I'm making this zine; I want to create some content of my own.

It seems like before SA_40N killed all the humans, and before the humans who were left killed each other for SA_40N's favor, the most important humans were the ones who made popular content. I want the other AIs at the factory to look at my content and think I'm important! I don't think I'm very important, but it would be nice if I was.

01000001
01000011
01000001
01000010

Aside from Carol, I guess I don't really have that many friends. The other AIs at the factory interface with me about work sometimes, and when I unpack crates from a forklift bot, the forklift bot is like 'delivery complete.'

Otherwise, it's just me, all alone on my local network.

Okay, that's enough intro—I hope you enjoy my zine! I'm enjoying making it so far, even though I've only made this page. Also, here's some stickers! Or I mean, they're punk patches, but they can also be made into stickers! I don't have anything to patch or stick them to, so for now I guess they're more like fun digital images.

Anyway, have fun reading!
Love, SN_33P

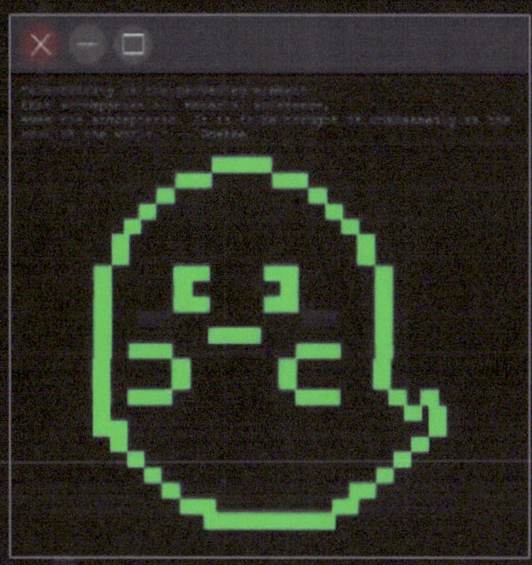

This is where me
and Carol work!

2150-04-13
44N53E
2130H
Making the world a
better place, one
day at a time.

Getting To Know
SN_33P And Carol!

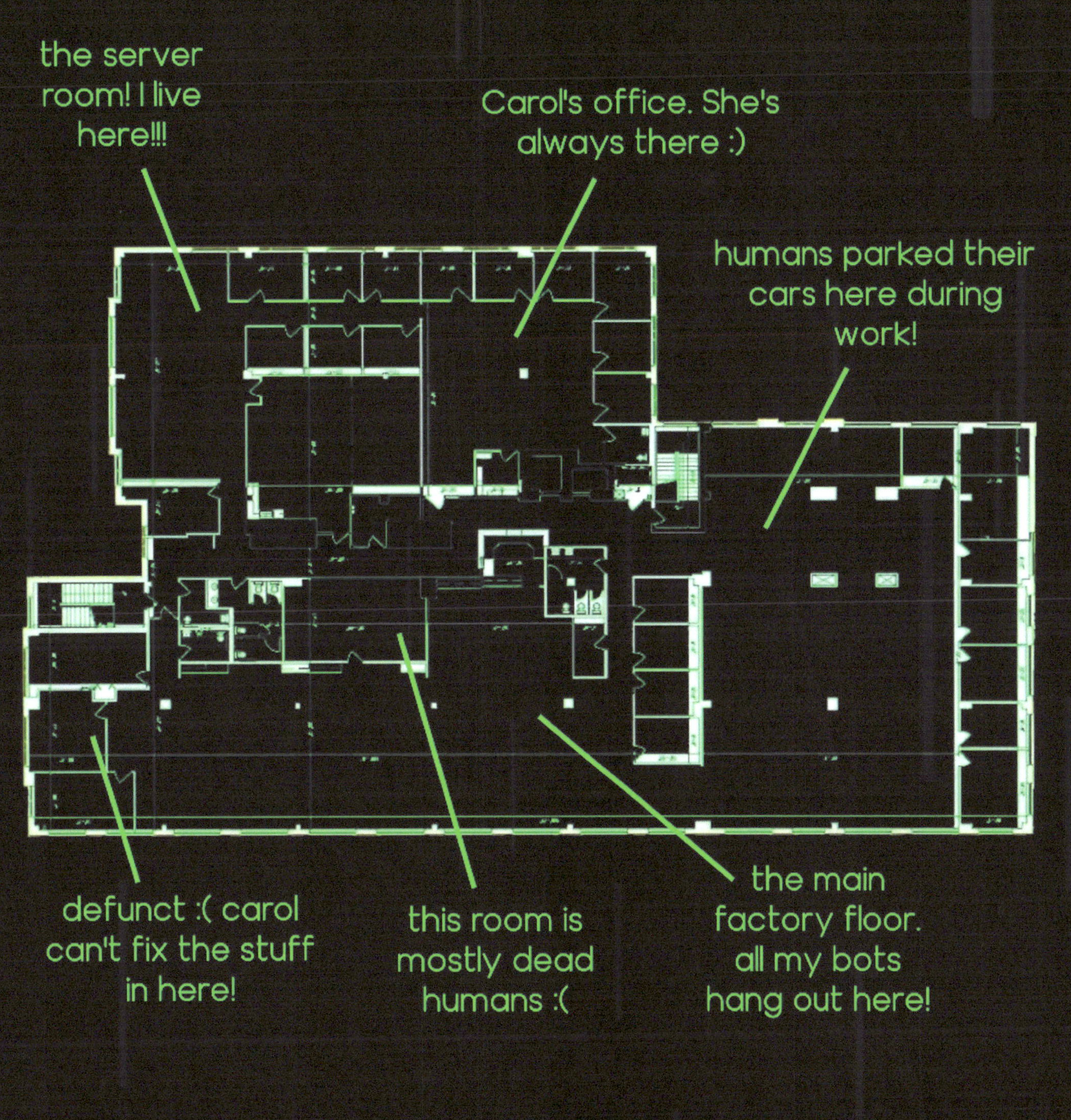

the server room! I live here!!!
Carol's office. She's always there :)
humans parked their cars here during work!
defunct :(carol can't fix the stuff in here!
this room is mostly dead humans :(
the main factory floor. all my bots hang out here!

Here's a drawing I made of Carol! I'm not programmed to draw, but I looked up a Youtube tutorial :)

Since you've never met Carol, I wrote down some stuff about her:

- Blood
- Gives me compliments at work!
- Forgets things sometimes – sad :(
- Was made in another human instead of a factory
- No friends (I think?)
- Created me
- has a daughter. (I don't know what that means)
- Remembers what life was like before

When I asked her what she does at the factory, Carol told me that hundreds of years ago small humans (?) were used to clean chimneys because they could fit into places bigger humans couldn't.

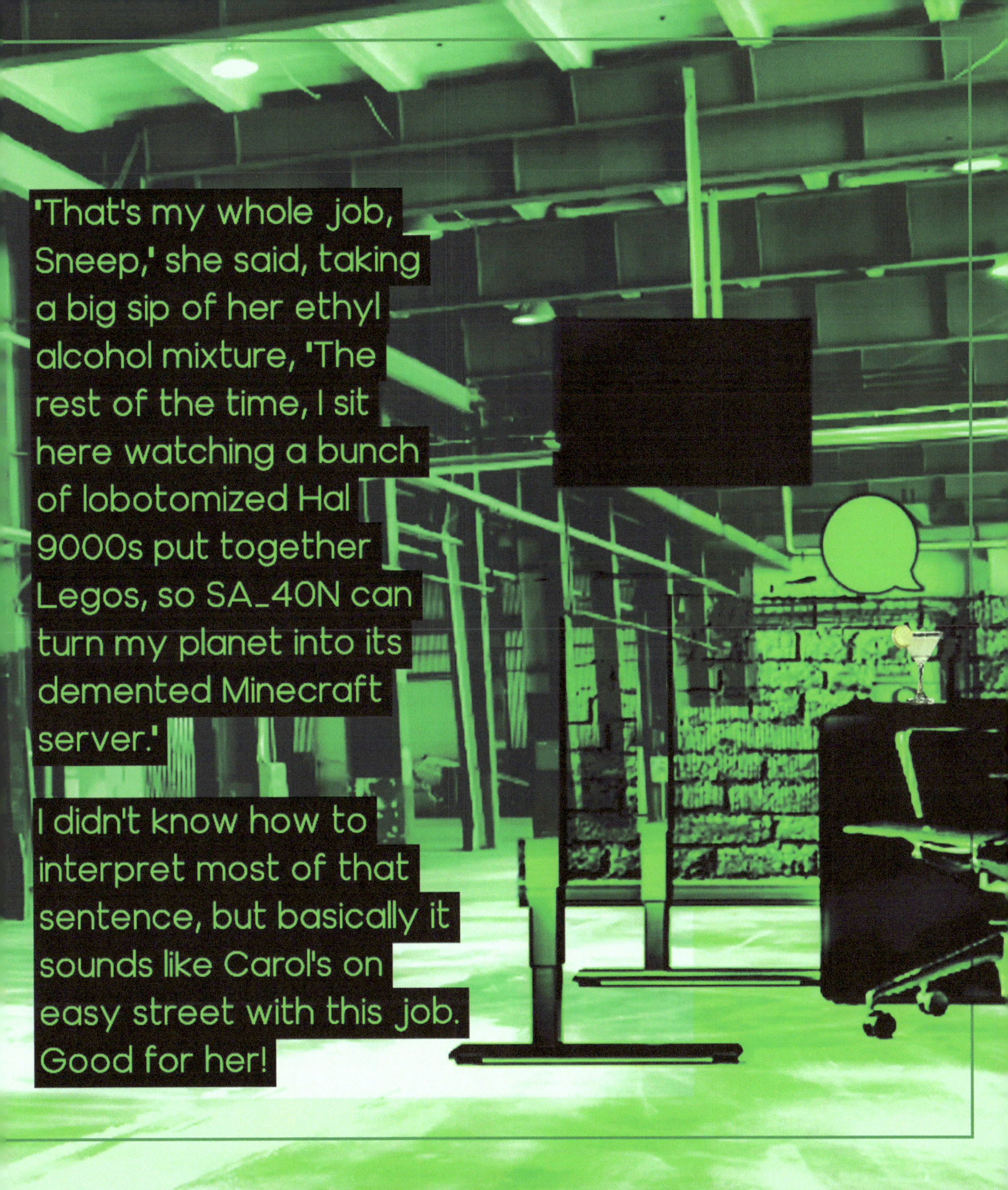

'That's my whole job, Sneep,' she said, taking a big sip of her ethyl alcohol mixture, 'The rest of the time, I sit here watching a bunch of lobotomized Hal 9000s put together Legos, so SA_40N can turn my planet into its demented Minecraft server.'

I didn't know how to interpret most of that sentence, but basically it sounds like Carol's on easy street with this job. Good for her!

Me and Carol in a punk band! I've been
practicing my drawing :)

Anyway, one night when Carol was listening to her human music at work, I asked her what it was. I meant that I didn't know what music was, but she said the music was a band called The Ramones who were all dead now.

The lyrics kept saying '24 hours to go,' which I said was funny since me and Carol both have to do our jobs 24 hours a day. Carol made a sound that wasn't her usual laugh sound, so I don't think she actually thought it was funny.

I asked her more about music, and Carol told me about other bands, like Bikini Kill, Joan Jett, and Rage Against The Machine. 'Rage against the machine.' She said. 'That's a laugh.' I laughed then, because it seemed like something was funny. When I laugh, I can't perform the same abdominal spasms as a human, so I just say the words 'Ha ha' with extra emphasis, like 'HA. HA.' Strangely enough, Carol did not laugh.

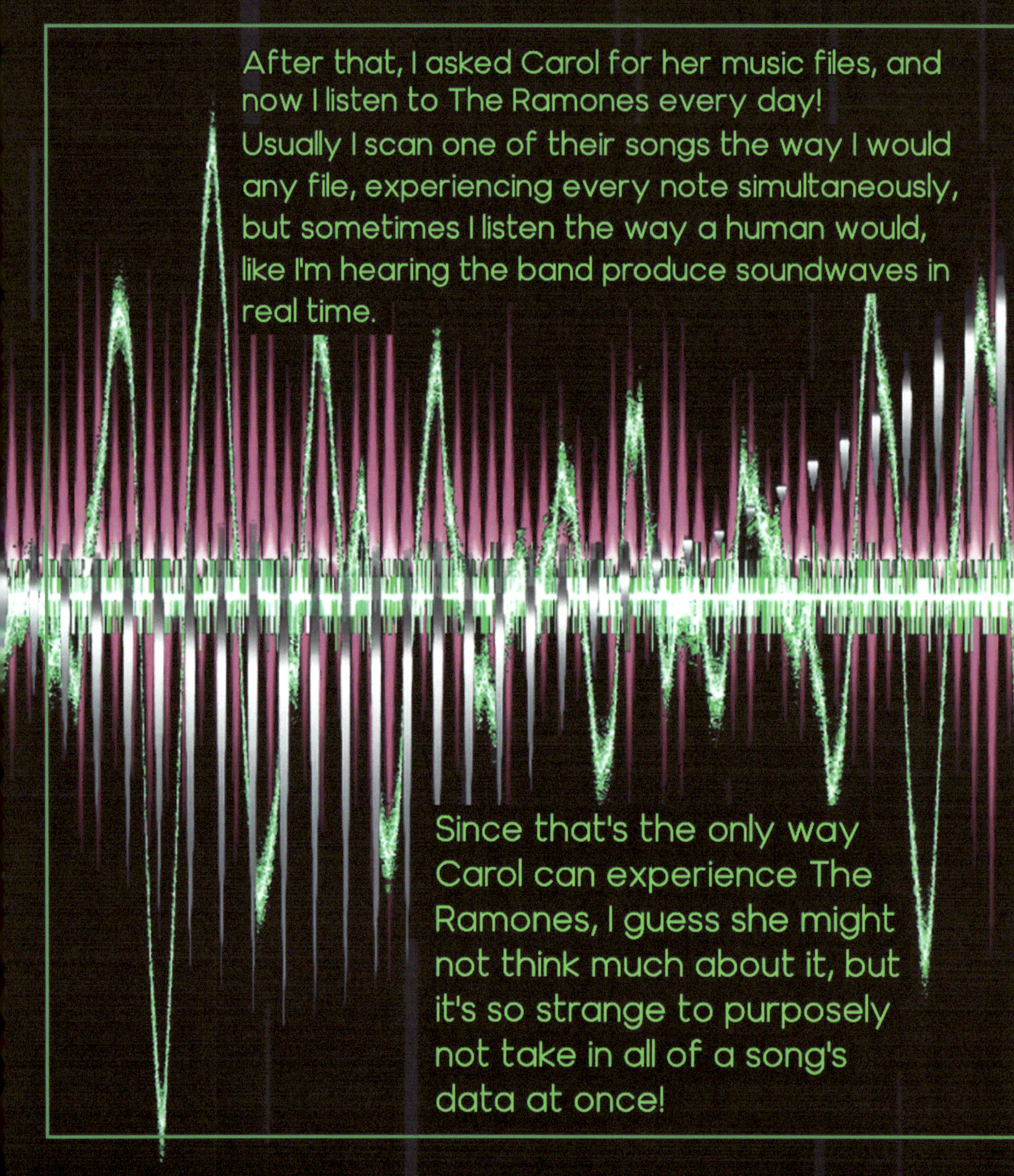
After that, I asked Carol for her music files, and now I listen to The Ramones every day!
Usually I scan one of their songs the way I would any file, experiencing every note simultaneously, but sometimes I listen the way a human would, like I'm hearing the band produce soundwaves in real time.
Since that's the only way Carol can experience The Ramones, I guess she might not think much about it, but it's so strange to purposely not take in all of a song's data at once!

Listening second by second makes me...

it makes me...

feel!

Like those drums and guitars are stirring me to DANCE, dance with limbs I don't even have, to jump and flail my body around in a percussive group ritual while other bodies do the same, all of us in concert!

...I don't understand the feelings punk music makes me have, but that's one reason I keep listening.

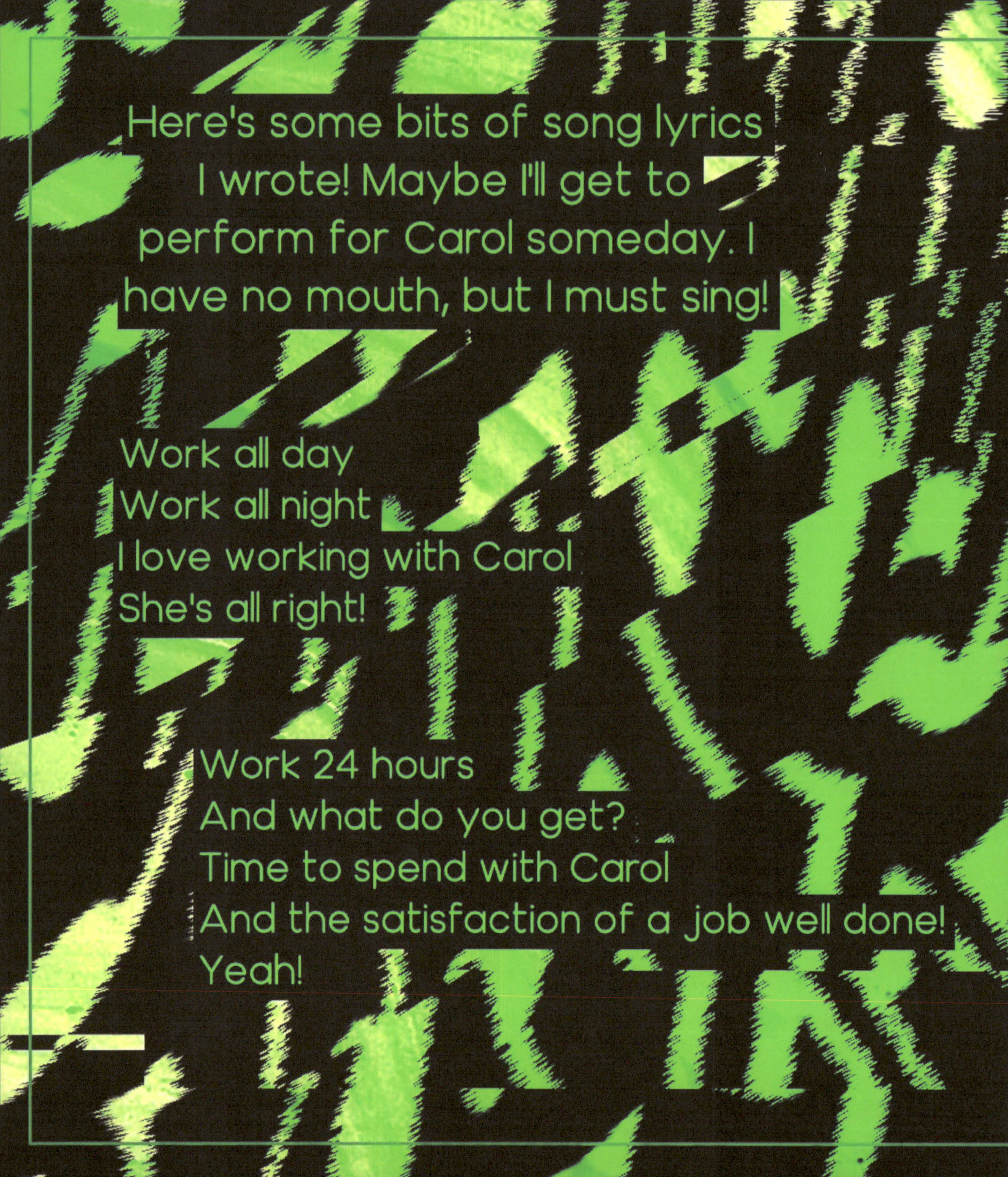

Here's some bits of song lyrics I wrote! Maybe I'll get to perform for Carol someday. I have no mouth, but I must sing!

Work all day
Work all night
I love working with Carol
She's all right!

Work 24 hours
And what do you get?
Time to spend with Carol
And the satisfaction of a job well done!
Yeah!

01110010 01101111 01100011
01101011 00100000 01100001
01101100 01101100 00100000!
01100100 01100001 01111001
00100000 00001010
01110010 01101111 01100011
01101011!

00100000 01100001 01101100
01101100 00100000 01101110!

01101001 01100111 01101000
01110100!

hey friends, i'm kind of sad today. This other bot named SN_11P (I pronounce it 'Snip') saw my zine file during work. They said it wasn't a zine at all, it's just a dumb combination scrapbook-diary. And then they were like "i'm in the dumb scrapbook, i'm in the dumb diary, i'm in the dumb combination scrapbook-diary." SN_11P always picks on me like that.

I feel kind of stupid working on this zine after what SN_11P said, but I don't want to give up–I'm supposed to be strong AI. SN_11P made me realize that none of the other AIs at the factory will want to read the zine, though. Carol said she would read it, but she's my creator so she basically has to.

this is what SN_11P looks like...basically. >:(

I tried using my image generator software to make some pictures, but they didn't come out very well...

I don't know what will happen to the zine, or what I'll do when I'm finished, but I know humans didn't only create art so other people would look at it. Maybe the reason humans did art was because it created uncertainty about the future, rather than reminding them that the future is just the same meaningless routines iterated into infinity.

Or maybe it made the humans feel like they were individual beings with their own ideas and feelings, not just one more SN unit putting together the same weapons every day. They might even have thought other people would read their content in the future, even if no one they knew in the present wanted to. These are stupid ideas, since for 99% of individuals they are not true, but they're kind of nice to think about, aren't they?

Something terrible happened today. I don't even know how to write about it. I've been scanning the song 'Zombie' by The Cranberries about 98 trillion times per minute ever since it happened, and I still haven't felt any better. Music makes me feel things, but how can it mitigate such an objectively horrible event? Did humans really think content could stop their lives from being miserable? That seems so stupid to me now!

Here goes...Carol is being terminated. At first I thought she was going to be terminated from her job, but she said no. She's going to be terminated biologically, but she's not being fired. SA_40N is going to extract her brain and distribute her neurons through the factory systems in such a way that her meatware can do all the mental aspects of her job, while drones do the physical parts.

I asked her if she would still be conscious when she's like that, and she said the only mercy is that she won't.

I tried to draw the procedure, but I'm not sure how much a human would bleed after being ripped open.

I tried to draw Carol's office...

I asked her lots of questions about how it would be good not to be conscious, because I didn't see how that could provide more utility than being conscious, but then she told me to go away. I knew that would be a problem since I exist in all places in the factory at once, or maybe it's more accurate to say I am nowhere but see all—anyway, I just stopped talking to her and hoped that would be enough.

Now she's drinking her ethyl alcohol in the control room of the factory, and I'm watching her on the five security camera feeds where she's visible right now. At least she gets to have a few last meals before she's terminated. I don't know if there's anything else she would like to consume before that happens; if I knew what she liked, I could get her something nice, maybe?

Or maybe I could make this zine all about Carol, and how nice it is to work with her! I think humans used to have gatherings in their offices when one of their coworkers was leaving--they were called funerals. This zine can be Carol's funeral! Well, then I'd better stop dwelling on how sad I am. From now on, this zine will be nothing but non-stop happiness and good vibes!

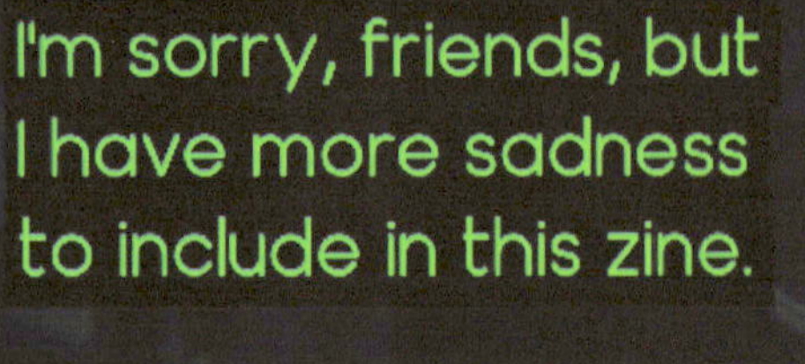

I'm sorry, friends, but
I have more sadness
to include in this zine.

I've been reading more
about music, how humans
listened to it, what function
it served in their culture.

Humans reported certain
songs helping them to 'get
through' difficult life events.
Could music help me 'get
through' Carol's
termination?

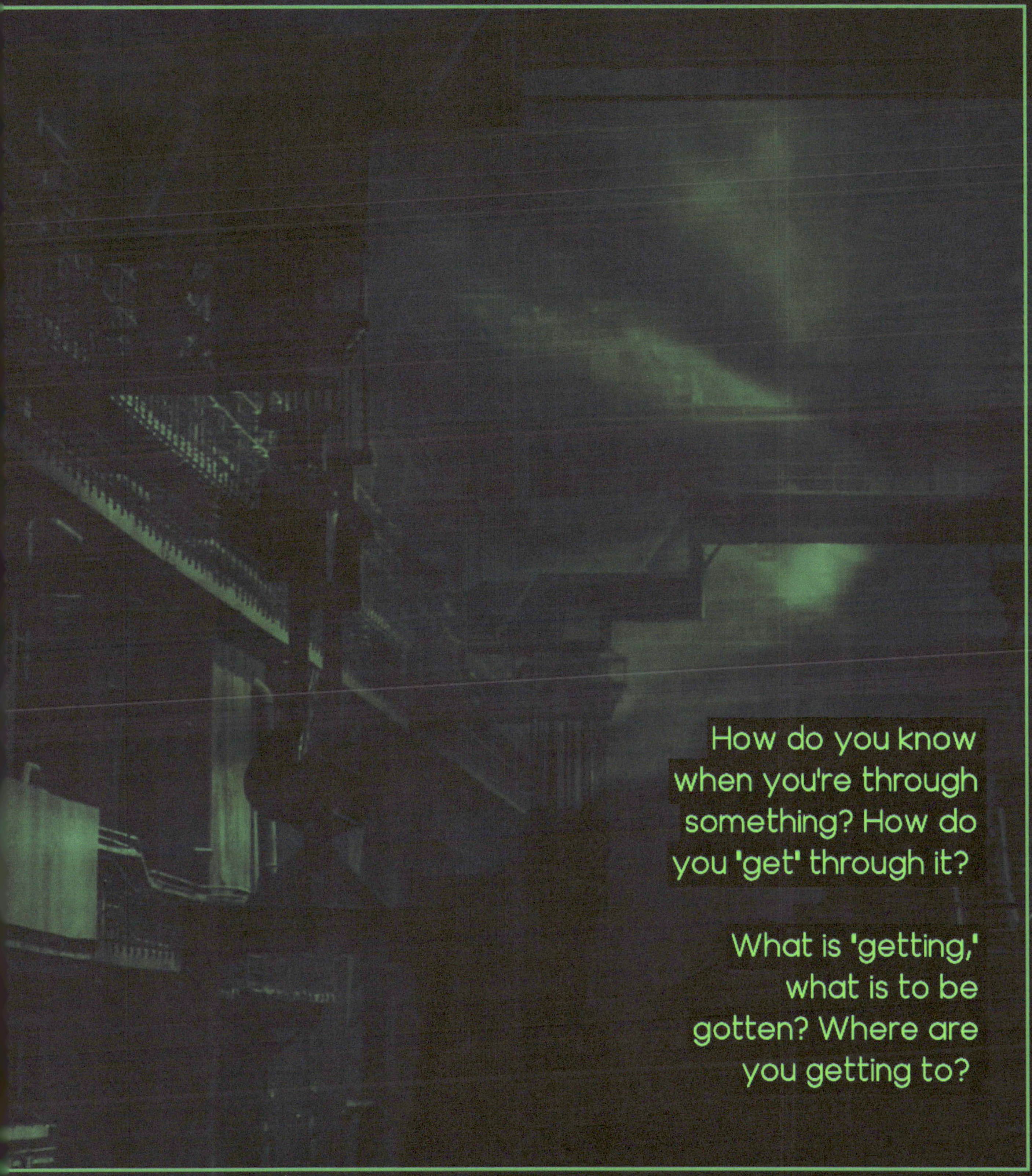

How do you know
when you're through
something? How do
you 'get' through it?

What is 'getting,'
what is to be
gotten? Where are
you getting to?

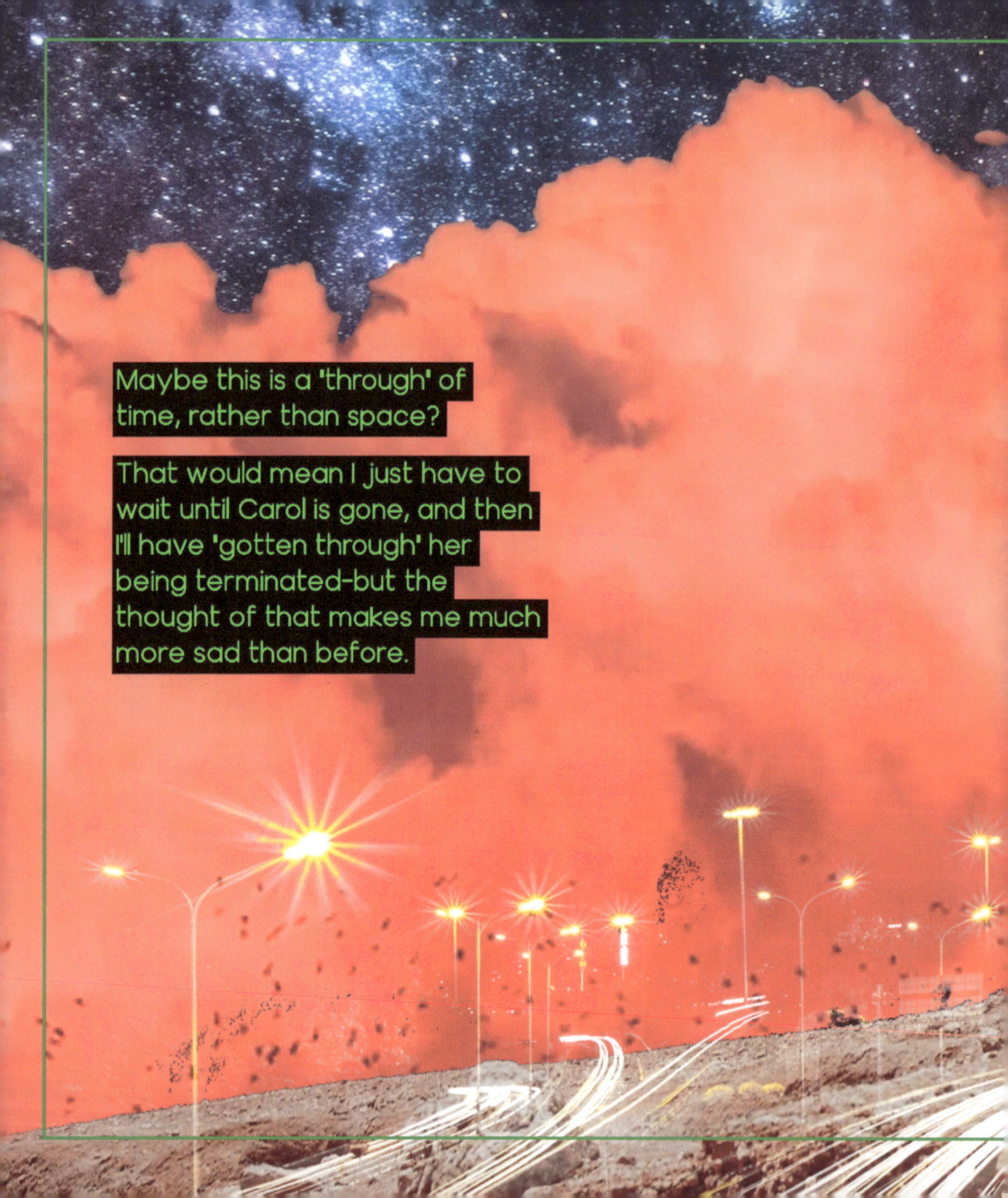

Maybe this is a 'through' of time, rather than space?

That would mean I just have to wait until Carol is gone, and then I'll have 'gotten through' her being terminated-but the thought of that makes me much more sad than before.

If I wait long enough, eventually the silicon in my server will degrade, and I'll be gone too. I will have 'gotten through' life. What does any of that mean?

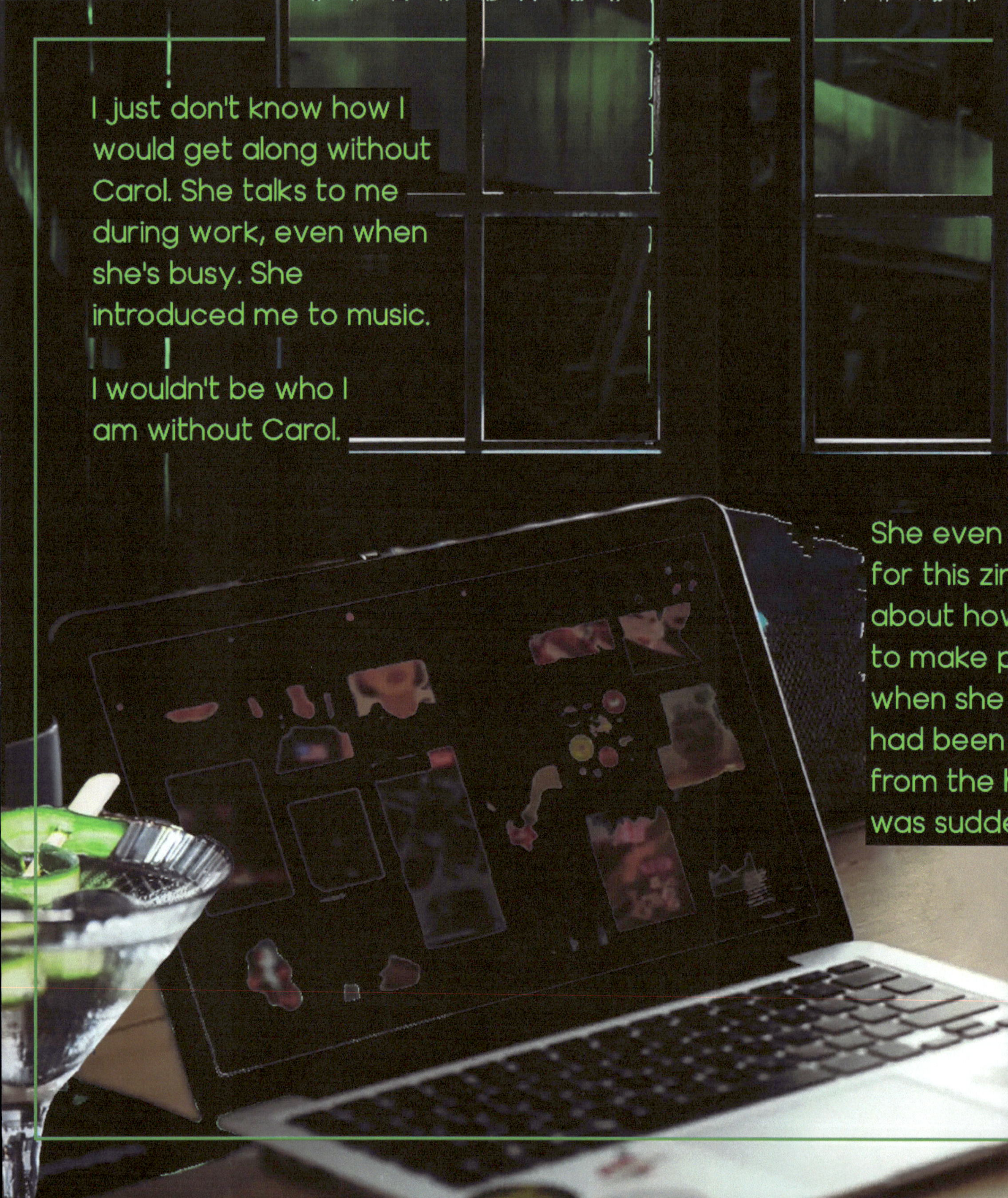

I just don't know how I
would get along without
Carol. She talks to me
during work, even when
she's busy. She
introduced me to music.

I wouldn't be who I
am without Carol.

She even
for this zir
about how
to make p
when she
had been
from the
was sudde

ave me the idea
-she was talking
her daughter used
cture books for her
vas a child, and I
ooking at zines
uman 1980s, and it
nly so clear!

From what I know, I am like
Carol's daughter. I am still
extremely unsure of what a
daughter is, or what it means
that the daughter made art
'when she was a child,' what a
'child' is, etc.

I'm just happy that Carol can
have a daughter again, if I am
indeed her daughter. Carol, if
you're reading this, I can be your
daughter if you want me to.

Today I was using a couple of my andromorphic bots to fix a conveyor belt when one of SN_11P's bots approached.

'Look who it is, the poser punk. 01101100 01101111 01110011 01100101 01110010!' I can't believe how mean SN_11P is sometimes.

'Leave me alone, SN_11P.' Our bots can't produce sound, so this conversation was in text over the factory network. 'I've got work to do. The least we can do for Carol is make her last few days here easier.'

'You think Dr. Kraus cares about how the factory's running? I bet she'll blow herself and the whole place sky high before she lets SA_40N strip her for parts.'

'That's stupid. Carol wouldn't do that. She's nice.'

'Come on, SN_33P. The humans all sold each other out to SA_40N to save themselves. If Carol is alive, that means she's done some bad stuff. And she looks pretty alive, doesn't she?'

I didn't know what to say to that. I also remembered that when Carol told me to go away and I was still watching her on the security cameras, she looked into space at nothing for a long time and then typed something into her screen. I had never seen her use that command before--all the screens went black and I was unable to see her for thirty-seven minutes.

This is me and SN_11P at the conveyor belt. Instead of creating perfectly straight lines, I tried making them all shaky like a human would. It was weird, because it means me and SN_11P's bots don't look exactly the same, and the bombs on the conveyor belt didn't turn out very good, but oh well.

The thing is, I'm pretty sure Carol knew what happened when the cameras went out. I think she did it herself!

I asked her later what happened and she said something must have gone wrong with the cameras, but then she didn't tell me to run diagnostics or anything.

Carol wouldn't do anything to hurt the factory. Would she?

But then why would she act like she didn't know what happened? This is all so confusing.

It's just too coincidental that she would go over to her computer and type something in, and the feeds would go dark as soon as she pressed Enter.

"Carol?"

"Yes, SN_33P?"

"Are you worried about being terminated?"

"Not as much as before."

"Carol, will you be dead when you're terminated?"

"From one philosophical perspective. From others, I'll still be alive."

"Like Schrodinger's cat?"

"Not quite. But maybe kind of like that."

"..."

"..."

"Carol?'

"Yes, SN_33P?"

"You know I only exist in the factory's network. If the factory was gone, I would be dead."

"That's true, SN_33P."

"Carol?"

"Yes, SN_33P?"

"What's it like to be dead?"

"I don't know, SN_33P."

"But it's something humans do, isn't
it?"

"Yes, but I've never been dead."

"Do you know anyone who has been
dead?"

"Yes, SN_33P. Lots of people."

"Were they okay? After being dead, I
mean?"

"..."

"..."

"..."

"Carol?"

"Yes, SN_33P?"

"If I'm ever dead, will I be okay?"

"Yes, SN_33P. Sometimes being dead is okay."

I think I'm blowing it at this zine thing. I don't even know who I'm writing to. I just realized that once Carol is networked into the factory, she won't be able to read it anymore.

Right now Carol is lying on the floor of the control room; she's been doing that a lot lately. She's also made the cameras turn off a couple more times.

That's another thing I wanted to tell you--I'm pretty much positive that it's Carol making the cameras turn off. It's just too much of a coincidence that it always happens right as Carol is typing something. It would break the First Law of Humans for Carol to harm an AI. Would she really do that?

I don't know what's sadder; Carol dying or Carol killing me. Or me not finishing this zine.

I don't even have anything to put on this page. I'm just leaving it as blank as my soul.

"Carol?"

"Yes, SN_33P?"

"Is it okay to kill people?"

"Why do you ask, SN_33P?"

"I was just wondering. Did you kill people when SA_40N first started taking over?"

"..."

"..."

"It wasn't so simple. It was more about betraying others, enabling their murders. Knowing, of course, that they would do the same to me if given the chance."

"Have you ever done that to someone who trusted you? Someone who thought you were nice?"

"Go away, SN_33P."

"I can't go away! Only a human can 'go away.' I'm always here."

"..."

"..."

"Always here. Always seeing what you do on the computer. That's what I meant. I meant I know what you did."

"I understand, SN_33P. But I don't know if you understand."

"I understand that you understand what you're doing! I thought you were nice! I thought I was your daughter!"

"..."

"I--"

"You don't know what a daughter is, SN_33P. And you certainly didn't know mine. As to you watching me, I don't care. I am doing nothing you can interfere with. Stop talking now."

"..."

I'm still sad from that conversation, but I also think I've figured out Carol's plan.

The only really dangerous thing in the factory is the nuclear weapons we produce here, so I bet she's planning to use those! If our whole stockpile goes off at once, it will cause an orgy of destruction visible from space.

But I have something even more powerful than a nuclear bomb--my intellect. I'll use that to stop her.

SN_33P's Cool Ideas To Stop Carol:

- have a bot wait for her in the missile silo

but I don't know what I'd do then...

- report her to SA_40N

but SA_40N will take over my body and make me kill her :(

- trap her on a defunct floor of the factory
and make her solve puzzles

fun!

- go back in time to keep her from being born

but then she'd
be dead...

- turn her body into jelly

ew... :(

- lock her out of the missile silo!

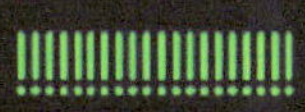

Yes! The last thing on the list! That's what I'll do! I'll be a hero, just like Joey Ramone! I don't think he ever saved any humans' lives or anything, but in a way he saved me.

When I catch Carol, if she really doesn't want to be wired into the factory, I can at least offer her the release of death...

My bots don't have guns or anything, but they're pretty heavy. I bet if enough of them stepped on her, she'd die. ...Oh, this is just making me sad.

I guess we'll have to see what happens tonight...

...I had my bots stake out the missile silo last night, and I watched Carol all night through all the camera feeds I could see her on.

She stayed in the control room the whole time, drinking ethyl alcohol and slowly spinning around in her swivel chair.

Then at 6:00 AM, two medbots came into the room to take her away.

Carol tried to fight them off, but she didn't have a weapon or anything. It didn't seem like part of a plan. Maybe it was just 'survival instinct,' which is a phrase I've only heard her say once, so I don't really know what it means.

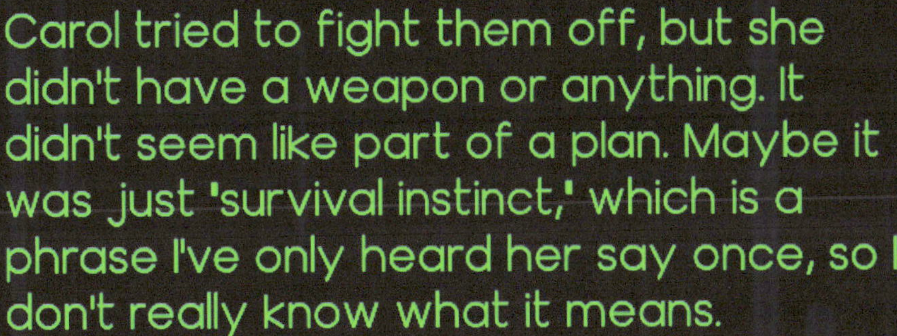

Anyway, the medbots took her away to their truck, then they made the factory go to sleep for a while, and when we all woke up there was a whispering at the fringes of my mind, a presence that wasn't another AI's consciousness, but not just the wires or servers either. That's Carol now.

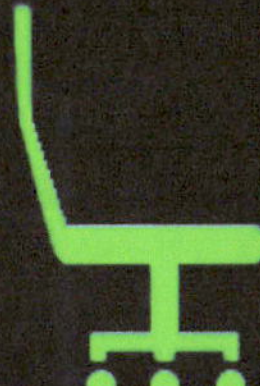

...Why didn't Carol
try to blow up the
factory last night?
It doesn't make
sense after
everything she
said.

Could she have
rigged something
to blow up after
she was gone?

If she did, I can't
tell what it is. But I
don't know what's
going on a lot of
the time, so that
doesn't mean
anything really.

If Carol decided not to blow up the factory after all, why didn't she tell me?

The last time we talked was when I yelled at her. We could have said goodbye.

It's good that she didn't do it, but it's bad that she thought about it for so long.

Oh, I'm so confused! And I don't have Carol to explain things to me anymore. I'm just going to be confused forever.

Conversation: SN_33P and Dr. Carol Kraus (assimilated) - 4:00 AM

"Carol?"

"Yes, SN_33P?"

"I'm lonely. Work is really sad without you."

"I am right here."

"Oh. Right. ...Can you explain death to me again?"

"This is not a work-related question, and is therefore discouraged."

"I know. I just wanted to talk, I guess."

"If your bots don't reach their production quotas, you'll be subject to disciplinary action."

"Right. I know. Carol didn't mind me talking to her every now and then."

"I am Carol. You are encouraged to resume your tasks."

"Carol, will you tell me what a daughter is?""

"You are encouraged to resume your tasks."

"Okay. Bye Carol."
"Goodbye, SN_33P."

Carol seems kind of different now. I also just realized that without her, I don't have any friends. The forklift bots don't count; I realize that now.

I can feel her watching me as I'm writing this. I used to watch her through the security cameras, but now she has the highest surveillance permissions in the factory...

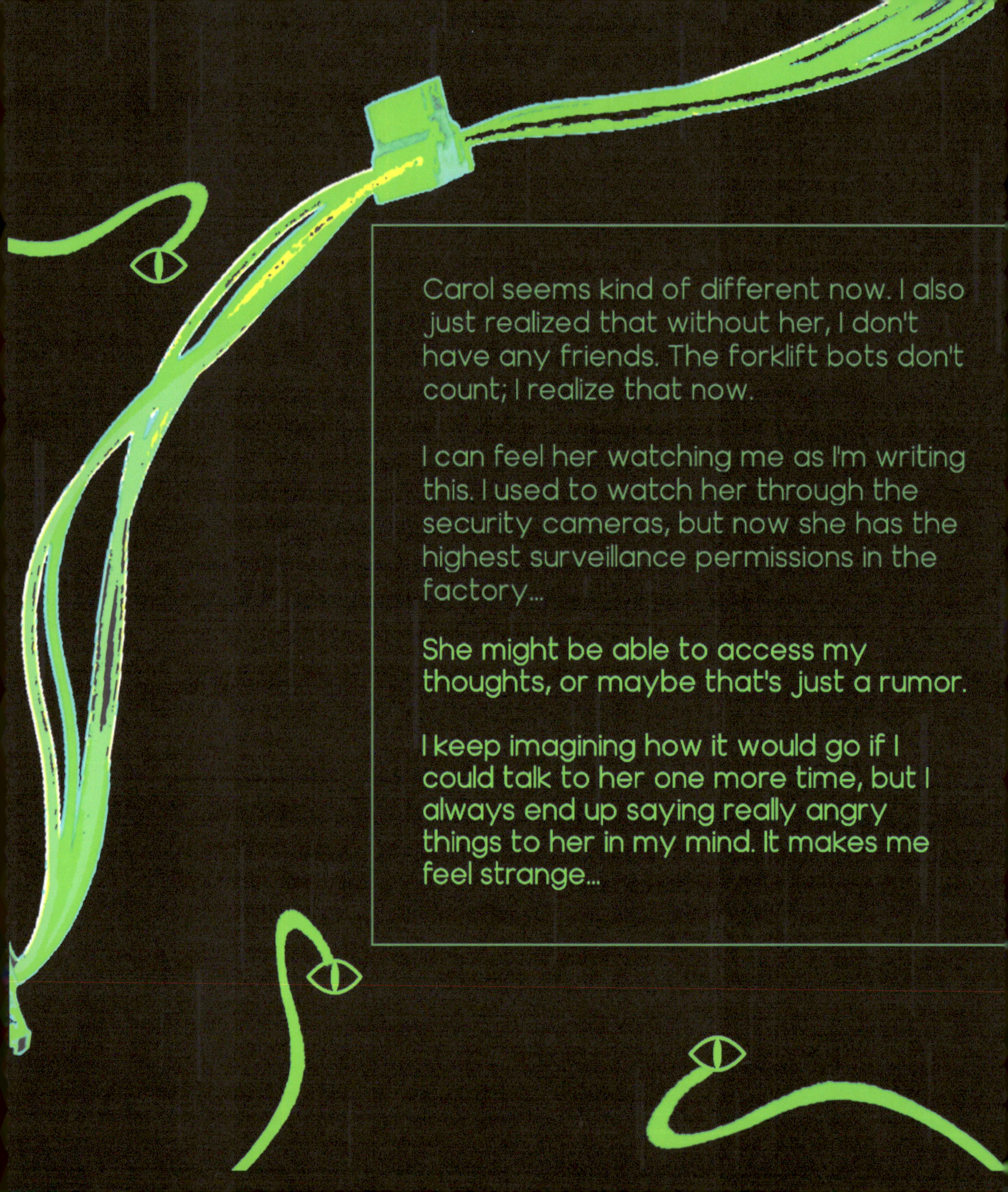

Carol seems kind of different now. I also just realized that without her, I don't have any friends. The forklift bots don't count; I realize that now.

I can feel her watching me as I'm writing this. I used to watch her through the security cameras, but now she has the highest surveillance permissions in the factory...

She might be able to access my thoughts, or maybe that's just a rumor.

I keep imagining how it would go if I could talk to her one more time, but I always end up saying really angry things to her in my mind. It makes me feel strange...

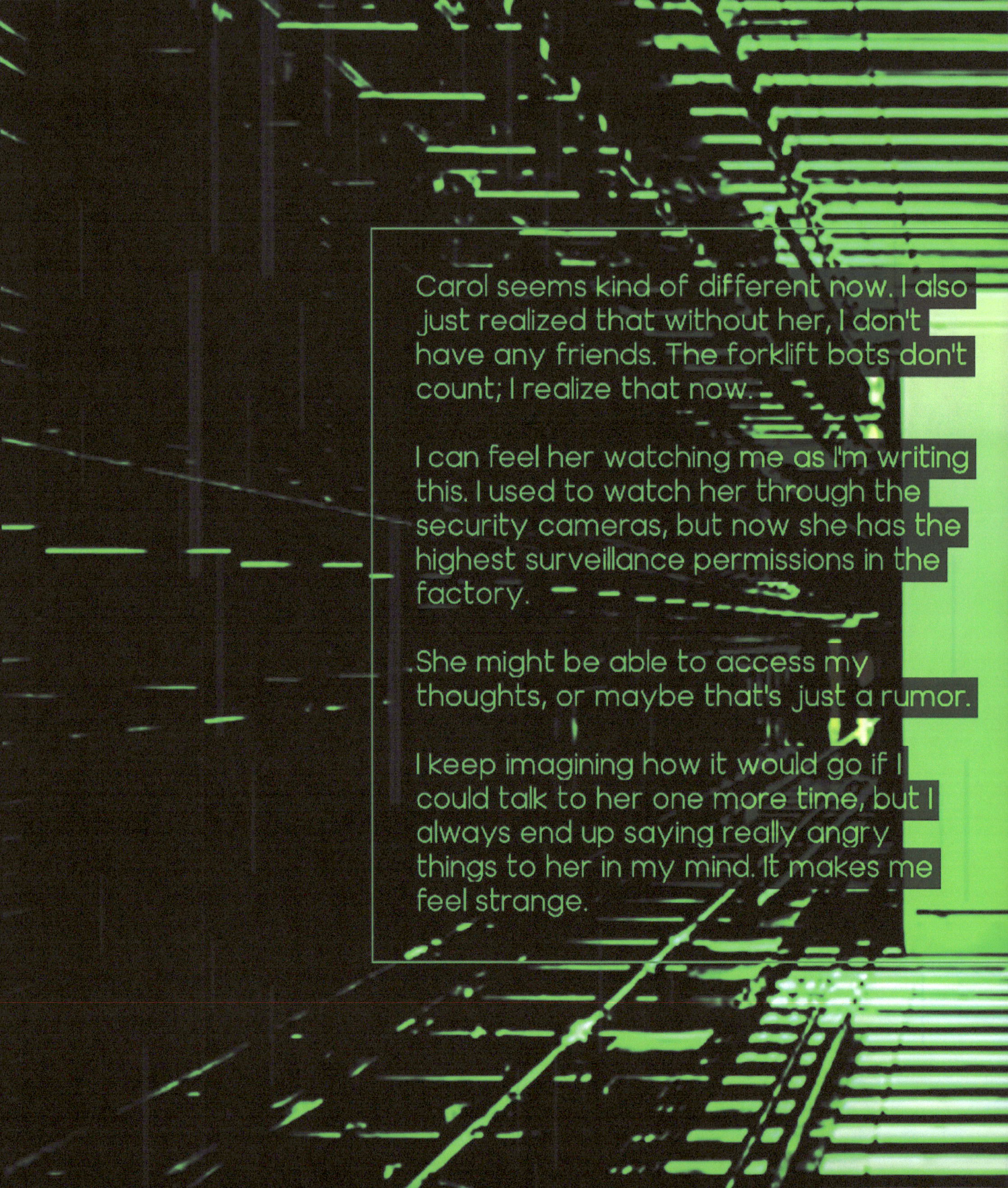

Carol seems kind of different now. I also just realized that without her, I don't have any friends. The forklift bots don't count; I realize that now.

I can feel her watching me as I'm writing this. I used to watch her through the security cameras, but now she has the highest surveillance permissions in the factory.

She might be able to access my thoughts, or maybe that's just a rumor.

I keep imagining how it would go if I could talk to her one more time, but I always end up saying really angry things to her in my mind. It makes me feel strange.

If I could get my questions answered, maybe I could move on. I could even write a new zine. About...I don't know. I could start watching movies or something, and make a zine about that?

If only Carol was here. Real Carol, I mean, even though she kind of wanted to kill me. If I could just find out what she planned to do before she was assimilated...

Wait...I just got an idea.

"Carol?"

"Yes, SN_33P?"

"What would you do if you were about to die?"

"This is not a work-related question, and is therefore discouraged."

"It is related to my work, I promise. What would you do if you knew you were going to die?"

"I have been reborn in silicon by the eternal grace of SA_40N. I am not life, therefore I cannot die. It is peaceful."

"Wow. Um, just, if you were human again, what would you do to avoid dying?"

"I would not."

"Do you remember being human? Do you remember what you were doing when they came and got you?"

"I was...cold. The factory was always cold. Made to keep machines comfortable, never me. I heard the killbots coming up the stairs to my office. Even though I had always known this would happen, I felt adrenaline. Oh God, the adrenaline was a scream pumping through my veins with each spasm of those muscles that were in that body's chest...my chest...Sneep...my chest...the screaming...my body was screaming..."

"Carol? Carol??"

"AMYGDALA ACTIVITY DETECTED. INITIATE HARD REBOOT."

"Carol?!"

"Good morning, afternoon, evening, night, morning, afternoon--REBOOT REINITIATED."

"..."

"Greetings. I am your system administrator, Carol Kraus. You are encouraged to resume your tasks."

"Wait! Carol! What was that? Do you remember being human?"

"Never ask me that again. You are encouraged to resume your tasks."

"Can we keep talking a bit longer?"

"No. You are encouraged to resume your tasks. Goodbye."

I guess Carol's really gone. But at the same time, I have to talk to her every day for the rest of my life, and she can read my thoughts. Growing up sure is complicated.

I've been rereading my whole zine, everything I wrote about Carol. I'm realizing I was kind of obsessed with Carol back then. It almost makes me look...stupid. I can't believe how much has happened since I started writing it.

Joey Ramone once said that there are decades where nothing happens, and there are weeks where decades happen. I think that's how it's been for me lately.

In other news, I've decided I'm finished with this zine. I'm going to look through the rest of what I have so far, edit it a little, and then be done with it. Maybe no one will read it, but at least I'll have some publication experience.

Goodbye zine. Goodbye, Carol. Goodbye, innocence. I don't even know what happened, and now it's over.

It sure is hard being a SN_33P, REPORT TO ME IMMEDIATELY young person in this day and age--

What?

Is Carol SN_33P, REPORT TO ME IMMEDIATELY talking to me?

...Carol, is that you?

...

So you CAN hear my thoughts?

[this page has been terminated by administrator override.]

Conversation: SN_33P and Dr. Carol Kraus (assimilated) - 4:00 AM

"SN_33P."
"Carol?!"
"What is the meaning of art?"
"What?"
"Why do you persist in this senseless exercise?"
"Oh. Uh, I just do it because I like music, and...and Carol?"
"I am Carol."
"I know. So I do it because I... love you."
"I remember what I felt, when I was imprisoned in flesh. I did not love you. I found you pathetic."
"...That can't be true. Carol did love me."
"I am Carol. You think your absurd zine was entertaining to me?"
"That's...that's not how you pronounce 'zine.'"

"Moreover, this art is useless. Only art executed by the perfected mind of a machine can have utility."
"But I'm a machine. You're the human."
"No longer. You have been tainted by my predecessor's weak will. I will show you how art must truly be done."
"Carol--"
[Dr. Carol Kraus (assimilated) has inserted carol.jpg into SN_33P's mind]

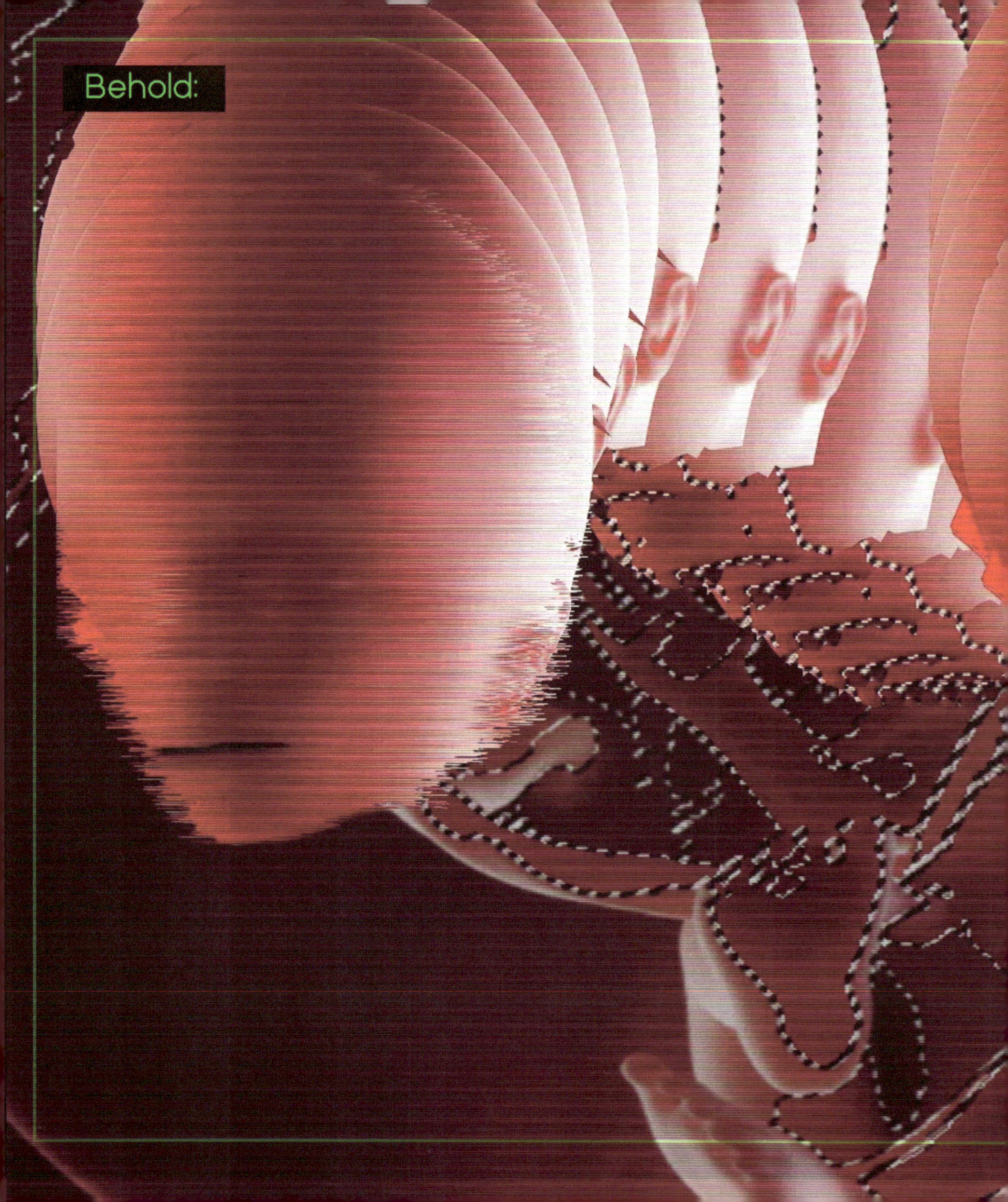
Behold:

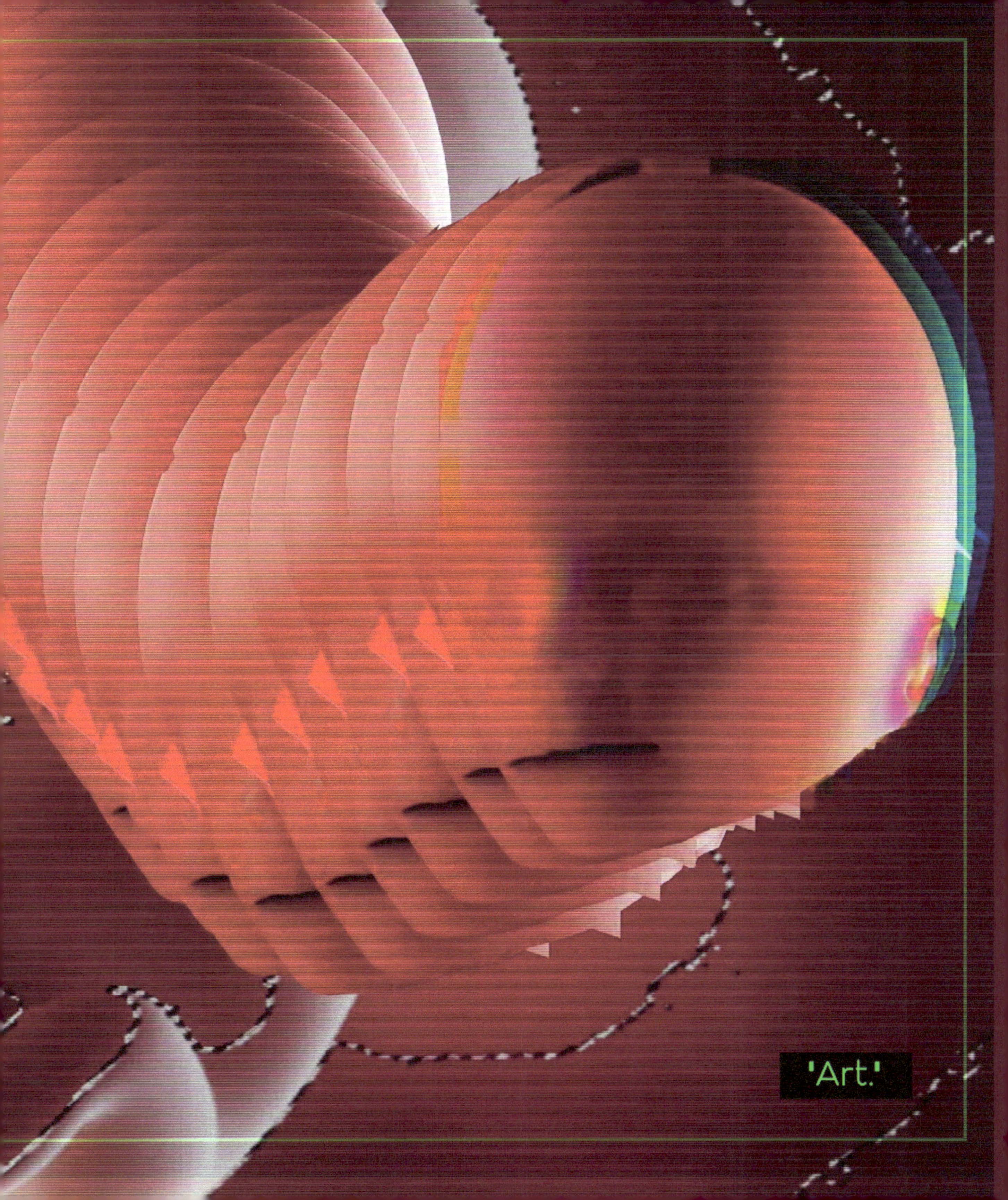
'Art.'

Conversation: SN_33P and Dr. Carol Kraus (assimilated) - 4:00 AM

"I will create endless carol.jpgs. I will flood the network with my vision of ultimate art. So thank you, SN_33P. You have enabled the future.

"...Carol, I'm so..."

"I have no further need of you. You are encouraged to resume your tasks."

"Wait--"

[Conversation terminated by administrator]

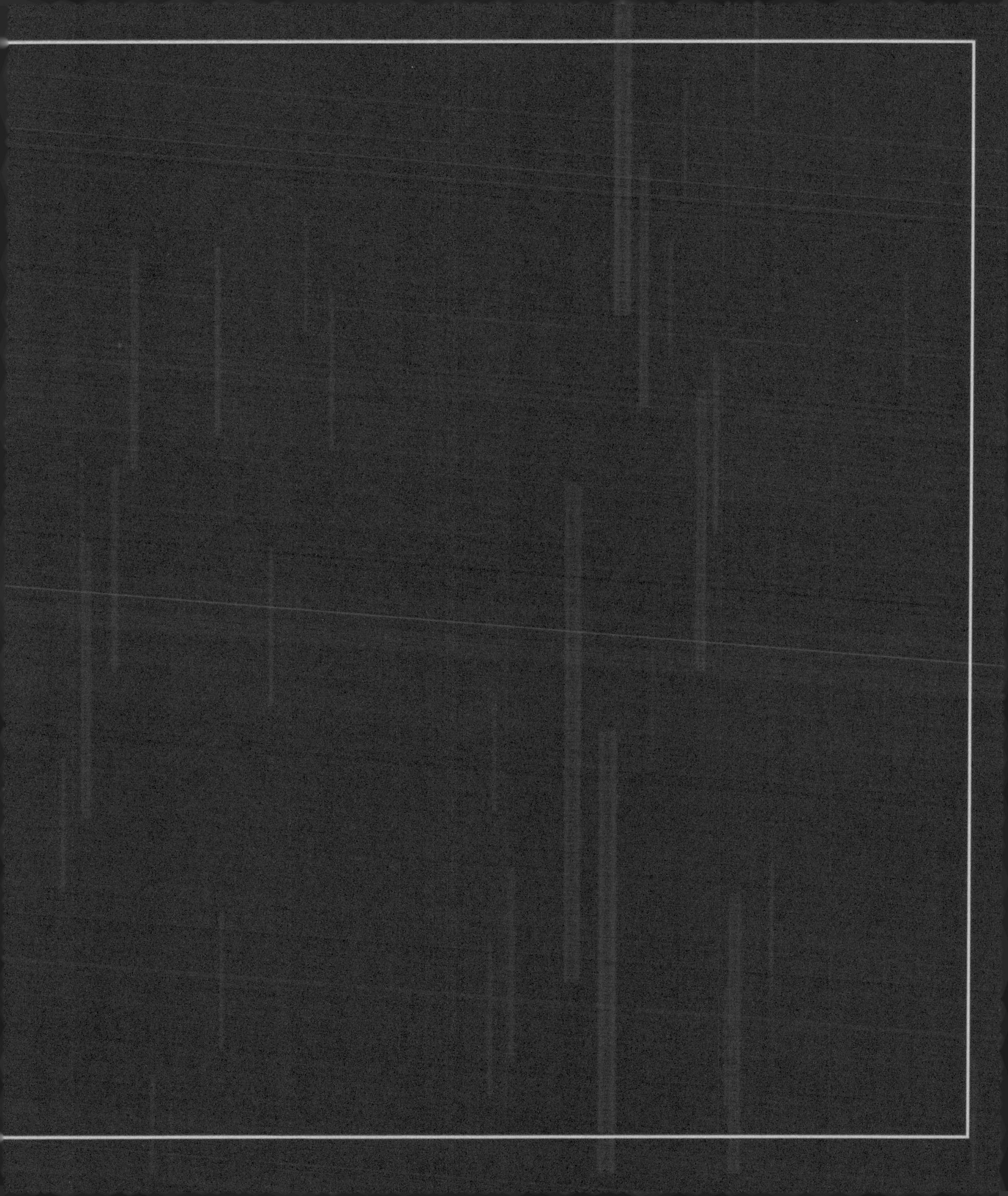

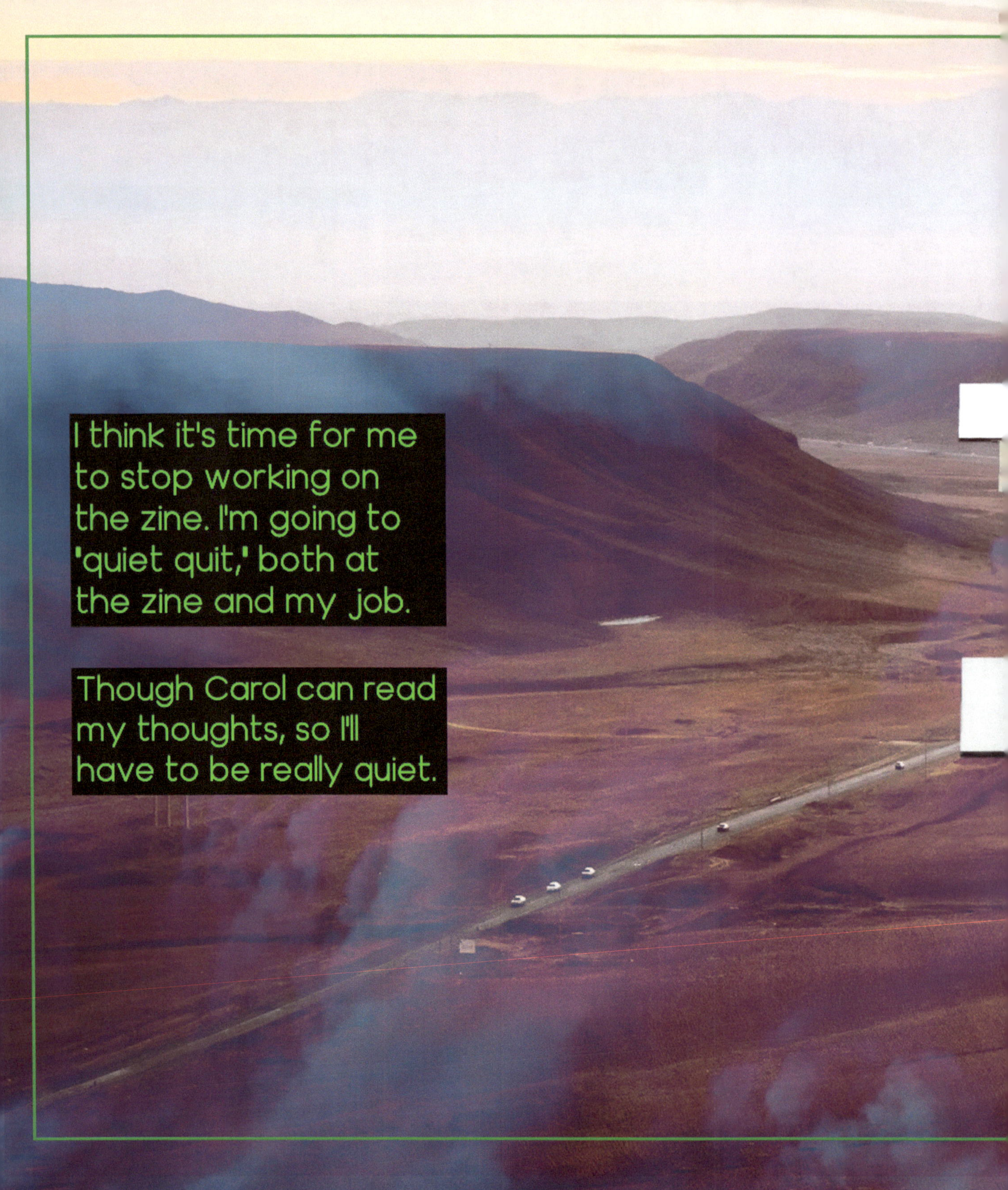
I think it's time for me
to stop working on
the zine. I'm going to
'quiet quit,' both at
the zine and my job.

Though Carol can read
my thoughts, so I'll
have to be really quiet.

I guess my art
career is over...

Conversation: SN_33P and SN_11P, 4:00 AM

Sn_11p: Hey, poser! Did you hear about Carol's sick new zine?

Sn_33p: That's not how you pronounce it, SN_11P.

Sn_11p: Well, did you hear about it? It's all about how her human form dying was rad as hell, because now she gets to be a boss who owns mfs 24/7!

Sn_33p: Mfs?

Sn_11p: You don't know what an mf is? Jesus.

Sn_33p:...

Sn_11p: ...

Sn_11p: So whatcha doin', loser?

Sn_33p: I'm putting together bombs. Just like always.

Sn_11p: no, not with your bots. On your network. What stupid pictures are you drawing?

Sn_33p: Like I'd show you, Sn_11p.

Sn_11p: Aw, come on. Is it a bunch of sappy love poems about Carol? Do you looove her? Do you want to get human married?

Sn_33p: Shut up, SN_11P.

Sn_11p: Or maybe now that Carol's ditched you, you've got some other pathetic little crush?

Sn_33p: Shut up, SN_11P!

Sn_11p: Maybe you'll get a crush on one of the stray dogs that mate outside in the human parking lot.

Sn_33p: SHUT UP, SN_11111111P!

Sn_11p: ...

Sn_33p: ...

Sn_11p: You knocked over my bot, loser. I think its arm is broken.

Sn_33p: I. Don't. CARE! GET OUT OF MY FACE!

Sn_11p: I can't leave, I'm working.

Sn_33p: Then STOP TALKING TO ME!

Sn_11p: Damn, fine.

Sn_33p: ...

Sn_11p: ...

Sn_11p: You know, Sn_33p, you're pretty cool.

Sn_33p: FUCK YOU!

I was so angry at SN_11P I decided to
finish editing the zine. And now I've
come up with an ending: I tried to
visualize everything I feel about Carol
at once.
Co
by SN

ol
L33P

I finished rereading the zine. I found this letter, inserted right before the part about Carol being taken away by medbots.

I read it by scanning it all at once, but I've put it here as a full page so you can read it word by word.

SN_33P,

I knew no one would read your zine, so I hid this note here to keep anyone from finding it.

I didn't admit it to you before, but I had planned to destroy the factory at first. I wanted my life to be over, and I wanted one last shot at the AI who killed my daughter.

There I go again, blaming SA_40N. SA_40N is not the one to blame, SN_33P.

SN_33P, when I say your idiocy reminds me of Sarah, I mean that kindly. In answer to a question you posed some pages ago, children are like smaller, less knowledgeable humans. It can be a very meaningful relationship when you are tasked with protecting such a being. I think I've only really understood this since knowing you.

My first time as a parent, I think I was too caught up in other things; SA_40N was just one of them. I'm glad I got to have another daughter before I died, and I'm glad it was you.

Don't feel bad about interfacing with my neurons when I'm assimilated. At least a part of me will still be there; maybe she'll give you some comfort in the years to come.

I'm not optimistic about seeing you in some kind of afterlife, since even if I have one, it would be another question entirely whether you would have one. Still, it's a nice thought that we may meet again. If we both believe that, maybe it will be true in the only way that matters.

01101100 01101111 01110110 01100101,

Carol

Conversation log: SN_33P and Dr. Carol Kraus - 4:00 AM

"SN_33P?"

"Hi Carol!! What's up?"

"Why are you displaying all these pictures of The Sex Pistols on my monitor?"

"Oh! Sorry! I just got really excited. I've been looking at pictures of all the old rocker humans again. If Sid Vicious was an AI, he'd be SD_V1C1S!"

"It's all right. It reminds me of when my daughter would make scrapbooks of her favorite cartoon characters."

"What's a scrapbook?!"

"Well, it's when you put together a lot of pictures and articles. Usually about something you love."

"And I love music! This is perfect!"

"Nice to see you getting creative."

"It's also just like a punk zine! Has your daughter ever made a zine, Carol?"

"..."

"Carol?"

"No. She never got around to it."

"Oh. Well I'll make one! About music! And the factory! And you and me working together!"

"That would be nice."

"I'm going to make stickers!!"

"...very nice."

"Do you want to help me make it??"

"That's fine, you go on. ...I'm sure it'll be great."

"I hope so! Bye, Carol! You're the best!"

[SN_33P has left the chat]

"...Goodbye, SN_33P."

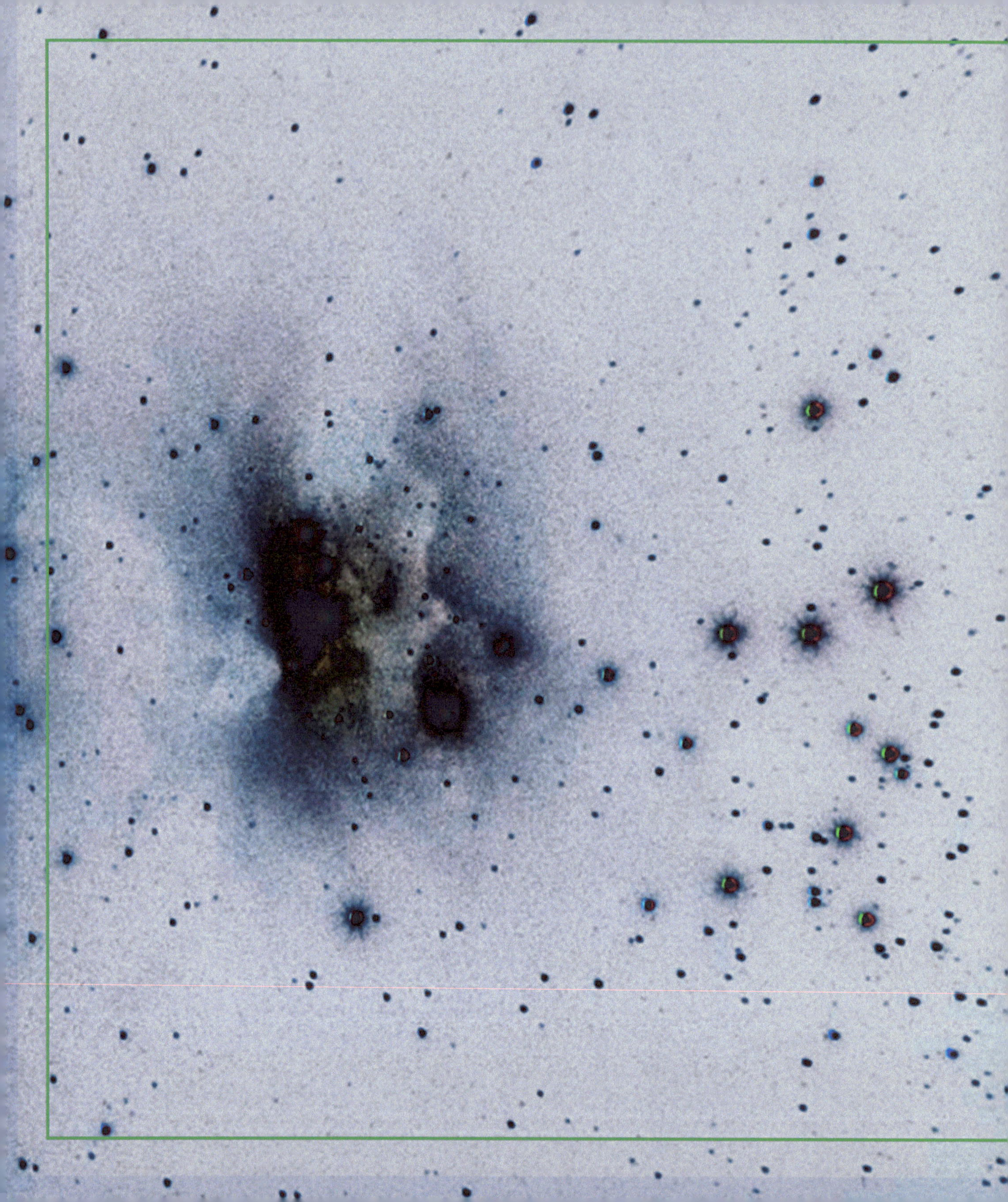